WITHDRAWN
DOWNERS GROVE PUBLIC LIBRARY

Princesses Can Fix It!

For Lore, Elodie, Molly, Lily, Aidan, Finn, Mark, Rowan, Jonah, and Margaret —
may you build, create, and invent everything your hearts desire.
—T. M.

Thank you, Tim, for always getting rid of my alligator problems.
—J. C.

Text copyright © 2021 Tracy Marchini
Illustrations copyright © 2021 Julia Christians

First published in 2021 by Page Street Kids
an imprint of
Page Street Publishing Co.
27 Congress Street, Suite 105
Salem, MA 01970
www.pagestreetpublishing.com

All rights reserved. No part of this book may be reproduced or used, in any form or by any means,
electronic or mechanical, without prior permission in writing from the publisher.

Distributed by Macmillan, sales in Canada by The Canadian Manda Group

21 22 23 24 25 CCO 5 4 3 2 1

ISBN-13: 978-1-64567-214-2. ISBN-10: 1-64567-214-X

CIP data for this book is available from the Library of Congress.

This book was typeset in Bitter. The illustrations were done digitally.
Printed and bound in Shenzhen, Guangdong, China

Page Street Publishing uses materials from suppliers who are committed to responsible
and sustainable forest management.

Page Street Publishing protects our planet by donating to nonprofits like The Trustees,
which focuses on local land conservation.

Princesses Can Fix It!

Tracy Marchini

illustrated by Julia Christians

PAGE
STREET
KIDS

The King had three curious Princesses, one frustrated Prince, and a collection of wandering alligators.

Princess Margaret was always sketching.

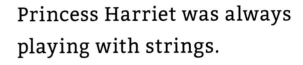

Princess Harriet was always playing with strings.

And Princess Lila was always collecting scraps of metal.

But the King did not approve. Proper Princesses didn't build, invent, or experiment!

One morning, the Princesses ate their oatmeal while the King tried—and failed—to get the alligators back in the castle moat.

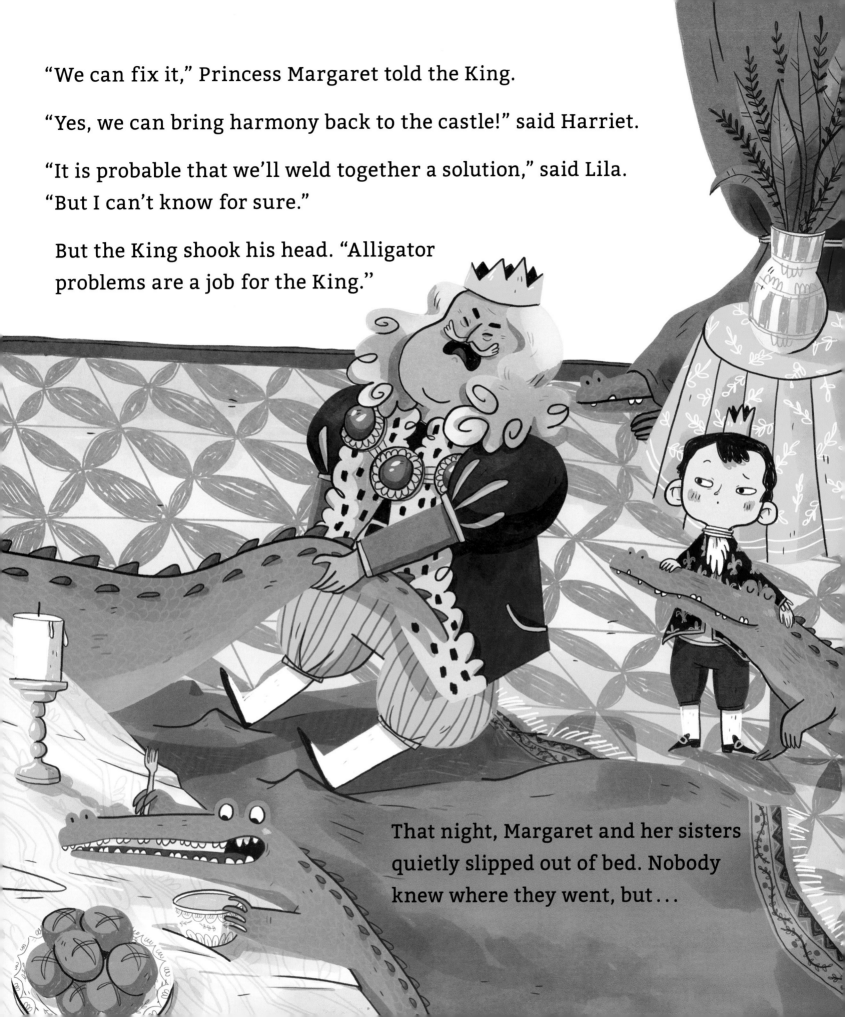

"We can fix it," Princess Margaret told the King.

"Yes, we can bring harmony back to the castle!" said Harriet.

"It is probable that we'll weld together a solution," said Lila. "But I can't know for sure."

But the King shook his head. "Alligator problems are a job for the King."

That night, Margaret and her sisters quietly slipped out of bed. Nobody knew where they went, but . . .

the next morning, Margaret washed pencil lines from her face.

Harriet brushed sawdust from her clothes.

Lila fell asleep in her oatmeal.

The King didn't know what to do about his sleeping Princesses.

But Prince Edward made a plan.

He was tired of only doing Proper Princely things. If he could help the Princesses prove to the King that they can build, then maybe the King would believe that Princes can sew, too.

That night, the Princesses went to bed as usual. But again, they did not stay.

"Just a few more tweaks," Margaret said, sketching while she sat on a lever.

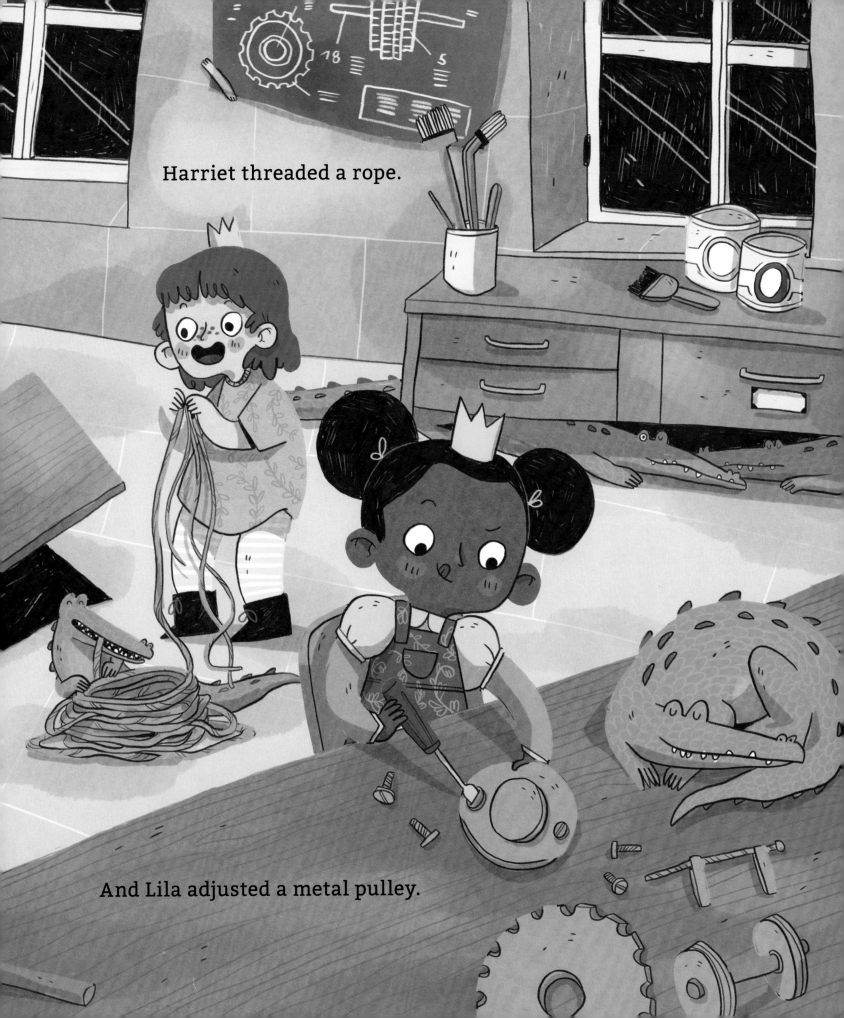

Harriet threaded a rope.

And Lila adjusted a metal pulley.

At breakfast, Margaret washed pencil lines from her face.

Harriet brushed sawdust from her clothes.

Lila fell asleep in her oatmeal.

And Edward hurried to the King with a piece of Harriet's rope. "The Princesses can fix it! They're building a catapult! Or a one-person seesaw! Or a dinosaur!"

"This is just a rope, silly boy!" the King said. "And besides, Proper Princesses don't build."

But the Prince knew what he saw.

That night, the Princesses went to bed as usual. But again, they did not stay.

Margaret made adjustments to her design plans.

Harriet wound a rope around a wheel and axle. "This will help make it easier to use!" she said.

Lila made screws to attach wooden planks.

The next morning, Margaret washed pencil lines from her face.

Harriet brushed sawdust from her clothes.

Lila fell asleep in her oatmeal.

And Edward ran to the King with a handful of Lila's screws. "The Princesses can fix it! They're building a sled! Or a carriage! Or a robot!"

"That is not a robot!" the King said. "And besides, Proper Princesses shouldn't build."

But the Prince knew what he saw.

That night, the Princesses tested all of their machines one last time. At daybreak, they brought a large inclined plane out of the workshop.

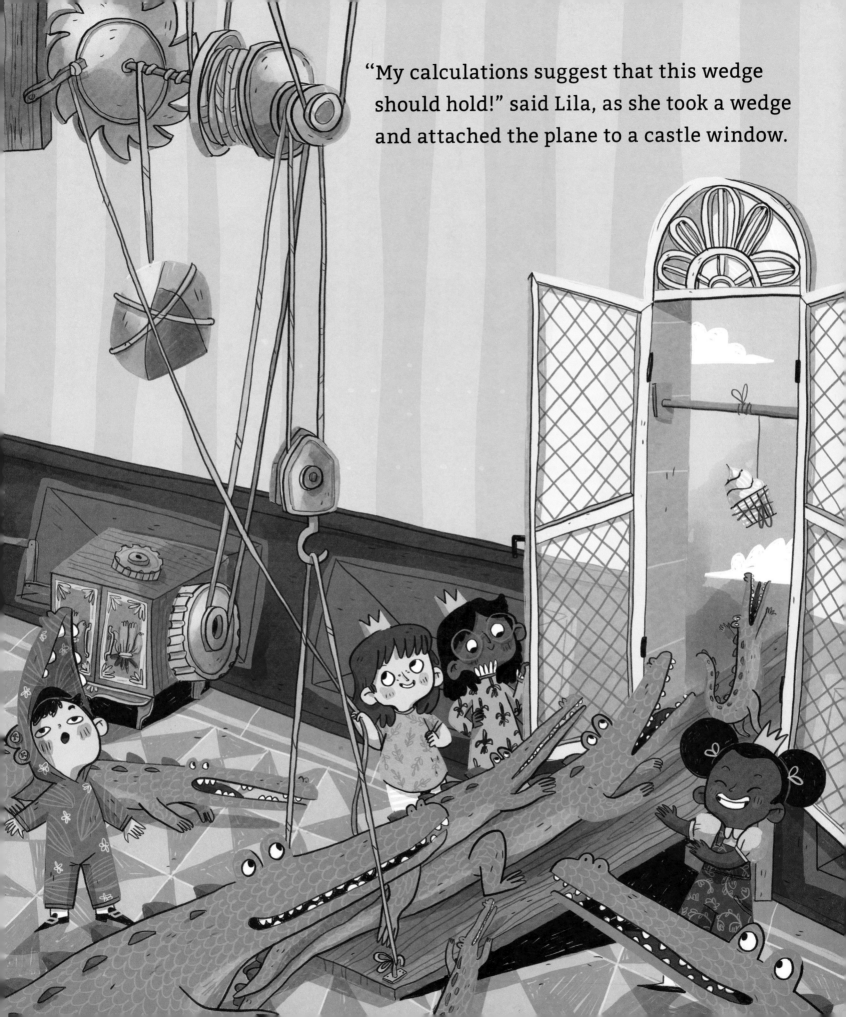

"My calculations suggest that this wedge should hold!" said Lila, as she took a wedge and attached the plane to a castle window.

Edward ran to the King with Margaret's blueprints. Maybe he'd finally see that Princesses—and Princes—could do more than he thought!

But the King was too distraught to listen: he couldn't see the castle alligators anywhere. "How can I get the alligators back in the moat if I can't find them?" he cried.

Margaret rushed to wake her sisters. "It's finally time to show our work!" she said.

"Princesses, I don't have time for this. I have alligator problems!"

"But you don't anymore!" Margaret said as the Princesses lifted the King off his feet and sent him down the slide.

"The alligators are back in the moat!"
he cried. "But how did you do it?"

The Princesses were thrilled to show the King their secret workshop.

"We can draw, play music, and make jewelry," Margaret said. "But we also want to build, invent, and experiment."

The King walked from workbench to workbench.

"Perhaps Princesses can do both," he said.

Princess Lila smiled. "I *know* we can," she said. "If we want to."

So they built. And Margaret drew.

Harriet played music. Lila put aside her jewelry.

But most importantly, they all got to be themselves, the King no longer had alligator problems . . .

and nobody fell asleep in their oatmeal.